A Night at the Zoo

by **Kathy Caple**

I Like to Read®

Holiday House / New York

To my husband, Walter

I LIKE TO READ is a registered trademark of Holiday House, Inc.
Copyright © 2014 by Kathy Caple
All Rights Reserved
HOLIDAY HOUSE is registered in the U.S. Patent and Trademark Office.
Printed and Bound in April 2014 at Toppan Leefung, DongGuan City, China.
The artwork was created with pen and ink and acrylic paint, on 140 lb. hot pressed Arches watercolor paper.
www.holidayhouse.com
First Edition
1 3 5 7 9 10 8 6 4 2
Library of Congress Cataloging-in-Publication Data
Caple, Kathy, author, illustrator.
A night at the zoo / Kathy Caple. — First edition.
pages cm. — (I like to read)
Summary: During a visit to the zoo, Pop and Sam grow tired but while they are napping, not only does
the zoo close for the day but the animals come out to play—with Pop's cell phone.
ISBN 978-0-8234-3044-4 (hardcover)
[1. Zoos—Fiction. 2. Zoo animals—Fiction. 3. Cell phones—Fiction. 4. Humorous stories.] I. Title.
PZ7.C17368Nig 2014
[E]—dc23
2013018853

"Hello," says Pop.
It is Mom.
"We will be home soon."

"I want popcorn," says Sam.

They are sleepy.

Sam and Pop nap.

The zoo is closing.

Ostrich likes the phone.

Parrot takes it.

He drops it.

Monkey gets it.

Then . . .

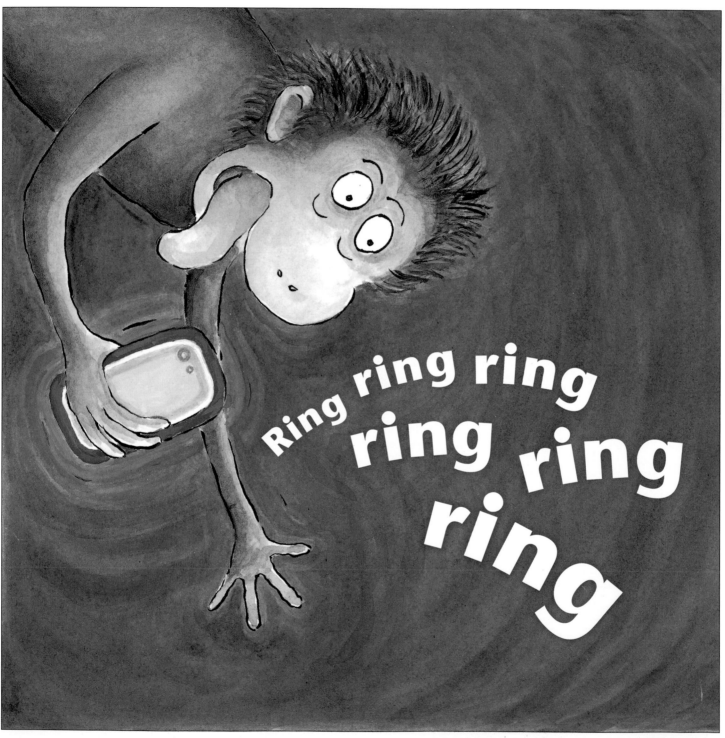

Monkey drops it.

Giraffe is dizzy.
He kicks Camel.

Camel is mad.
He kicks the can.

bam

bam

bam

Sam and Pop wake up.
A man comes.

"We fell asleep," says Pop.

Sam and Pop go out.

"Oh no. I lost my phone," says Pop.

Then . . .

The phone drops.

"Hi Mom," says Sam.

"What?"